For my grandparents: Angela, Guy and Mary

Brimming with creative inspiration, how-to projects, and useful information to enrich your everyday life, Quarto Knows is a favourite destination for those pursuing their interests and passions. Visit our site and dig deeper with our books into your area of interest: Quarto Creates, Quarto Cooks, Quarto Homes, Quarto Lives, Quarto Drives, Quarto Explores, Quarto Gifts, or Quarto Kids.

Inspiring | Educating | Creating | Entertaining

The illustrations were created in gouache and edited in photoshop
Set in Bembo Roman Infant

Published by Rachel Williams
Designed by Karissa Santos
Edited by Katie Cotton
Production by Jenny Cundill and Kate Riordan

Manufactured in Dongguan, China TL102018

3 5 7 9 8 6 4 2

MIX
Paper from
responsible sources
FSC® C104723
FSC
www.fsc.org

Silent Night

Lincoln
Children's Books

Silent night, holy night;
All is calm, all is bright,

Round yon virgin
mother and child.

Holy infant, so tender and mild,
Sleep in heavenly peace,
Sleep in heavenly peace.

Silent night, holy night,
Shepherds quake at the sight.

Glories stream from heaven afar,

Heavenly hosts sing
Alleluia!

Christ, the Savior is born,
Christ, the Savior is born!

Silent night, holy night,
Son of God, love's pure light.

Radiant beams from Thy holy face
With the dawn of redeeming grace,

Jesus, Lord, at thy birth,
Jesus, Lord, at thy birth.

Silent night, holy night,
All is calm, all is bright,

Round yon virgin
mother and child.
Holy infant, so tender
and mild,

Sleep in heavenly peace,
Sleep in heavenly peace.

About the carol

"Silent Night," or "Stille Nacht" was composed in 1818 in Oberndorf bei Salzburg, Austria. Legend has it that on Christmas Eve, Joseph Mohr, the Catholic curate of the town, found that mice had chewed away part of the church organ, meaning that it would be out of action for the midnight mass. Mohr desperately needed something for his congregation to sing, so he wrote "Silent Night"—simple verses inspired by a visit he had made that day to a mother and her sick baby. When he had written the lyrics, he ran round to his friend Franz Gruber, an organist, and asked him to write some music for it. The new hymn was performed that night at midnight, to music from Gruber's guitar.

Weeks later, Karl Mauracher arrived to repair the organ. When he finished, he stepped back to let Gruber test the instrument, Gruber began playing "Silent Night," and Mauracher liked it to so much that he took it back to his own village. There, two well-known families of singers—the Rainers and the Strassers—heard it. "Silent Night" became a core part of their Christmas season performance.

In 1834, it was performed by the Strassers for King Frederick William IV of Prussia, and he then ordered his cathedral choir to sing it every Christmas Eve. "Silent Night" has since been translated into more than 200 languages, including English in 1858. During the truce of the First World war on December 25, 1914, it was sung by soldiers on both sides of the trenches. Whether the tale of its origin is true or not, "Silent Night" is one of the world's most beloved carols today.

Silent Night

Silent night, holy night,
All is calm, all is bright,
Round yon virgin mother and child.
Holy infant, so tender and mild,
Sleep in heavenly peace,
Sleep in heavenly peace.
Silent night, holy night,
Shepherds quake at the sight,
Glories stream from heaven afar,
Heavenly hosts sing Allcluia!
Christ the Savior is born,
Christ the Savior is born!
Silent night, holy night,
Son of God, love's pure light,
Radiant beams from thy holy face
With the dawn of redeeming grace,
Jesus, Lord, at thy birth,
Jesus, Lord, at thy birth.